1 MONTH OF
FREE
READING

at

www.ForgottenBooks.com

By purchasing this book you are
eligible for one month membership to
ForgottenBooks.com, giving you
unlimited access to our entire
collection of over 1,000,000 titles via
our web site and mobile apps.

To claim your free month visit:

www.forgottenbooks.com/free756647

ISBN 978-0-483-82405-8
PIBN 10756647

✓

OUT ON THE WORLD.

A DRAMA

IN THREE ACTS.

—:◦:-:◦:—

With a description of Characters, Entrances, and Exits, and the whole of
the Stage business.

—:◦:-:◦:—

Entered according to Act of Congress, in the year 1880, by
A. D. AMES,
In the office of the Librarian of Congress, at Washington.

—◦◦◦◦◦— *No. 4039 L*

OUT ON THE WORLD.

Zq 093

CHARACTERS.

James Alden..*A sea Captain*
Edward Harold..*Mrs. Alden's rejected suitor*
Larrie Linegan...*A servant*
Zeke Crowell..*A country laborer*
Harry Mansfield..*Protege of Mrs. Alden*
Mrs. Alden..... ....*Capt. Alden's wife*
Nellie Alden...*Their daughter*
Biddy..*An Irish servant*
Mrs. Crowell...*Zeke Crowell's wife*

☞ Between the second and third acts there is supposed to be a lapse of twenty years. Different persons will be required to represent the characters of Nellie and Harry, who are supposed to be nine years of age in acts 1st. and 2d. There must also be an entire change of costume in all characters.

ACT FIRST.—The Abduction.

ACT SECOND.—In Captivity.

ACT THIRD.—Reunited.

Costumes.—Modern.

Time of representation.—Two hours.

LIST OF PROPERTIES.

Sofa, center table, news paper, pail, scrubbing brush, towel, table, dishes to set table, pipe, matches, bottle, broken jar with small package in it, blackwhip, a pair of steelyards, lantern, book, musket, stove, basket of potatoes, basket of chips, rope, orange.

OUT ON THE WORLD.

ACT I.

SCENE FIRST.—*New York. James Alden's residence on Madison Avenue. Doors, R. L., and C. Sofa left of C., on which Mr. A. is reclining, apparently absorbed in thought. Center table a little right of C., at which Mrs. A. sits engaged in reading.*

Mrs A. Why James, you have not told me a word about it I The paper states that your vessel leaves this afternoon for Liverpool.

Mr A. Yes, the Atlantic will leave to-day. I have been thinking very seriously of this in connection with another matter.

Mrs A. What is that, pray?

Mr A. That man Harold's actions disturb me lately. I have seen him prowling around our house, and passing by with such an appearance, that I begin to feel suspicious of him. He is a most notorious scoundrel, and he will avail himself of the opportunity while I am absent to make us miserable.

Mrs A. (*dropping the paper and appearing startled*) What can you mean? this man has never disturbed us I Why do you think so meanly of him now?

Mr A. He has never taken advantage of us yet, because, fearing the consequences, he has never dared. But now, that old wound, inflicted years ago—before we were married—seems to gall him more than ever before. You know what I mean. You remember he paid his attentions to you before my acquaintance with you, and you recollect also your refusal when he offered you his hand. Every since this, he has sworn vengeance upon you, and after I had won you, this feeling of revenge was aroused to a still higher pitch, and I fear the villain has some new object in view. He intends to inflict some injury upon you or our daughter. (*Mrs. A. alarmed*) He knows how great is the attachment existing between us and our daughter, and I apprehend he has some plan by which he will deprive us of her.

Mrs A. I had never before thought of this; never considered him so base as that.

Mr A. He is one of the most artful rascals with whom the police of our city have ever had to deal. He is the most daring in his plots, and the most difficult to be detected in his operations. But my call at Liverpool is imperative. Keep a sharp look-out on this man; at the same time, let your watch over our Nellie be constant. Keep her with you. You will never be obliged to remain alone, as Larrie, who has always proved himself so faithful in his duty, will ever be ready to render assistance. Before I leave I will warn the police to watch carefully our dwelling, especially at night. I must leave you a little while, as it is necessary that I should go down to the boat to give directions concerning our departure. (*puts on hat, exit* L.

Mrs A. I have seen Harold very frequently, but I never detected anything unusual in his appearance. I saw him only this morning. He seemed to be deep in thought, but that is his usual custom. Mr. Alden is extraordinarily fearful. He is always just so apprehensive of danger every time he leaves; but nothing dreadful has occurred so far, and I have good reason to think nothing will.

Enter Nellie, R. *She is a young girl nine years of age.*

Nel. O, mother, just look here! See what I have got! (*holds out a large orange*) As I was swinging on the front gate, a gentleman was passing, and he took this orange from his pocket and gave it to me. Isn't it nice?

Mrs A. A gentleman gave it to you! Who can it be! Did you know him?

Nel. No I have seen him a great many times, but I don't know his name.

Mrs A. How does he look?

Nel. Well, he was rather tall, wears a great black beard, a tall hat, has got sharp black eyes, and carries a cane.

Mrs A. Why, that is Mr. Harold. (*aside*) There, I knew Mr. Alden's suspicions were groundless. Instead of using means to injure our Nellie, Harold seems to take a great interest in her, and his fondness for her is shown by this very act. It will not do to let Mr. Alden know this, for it will only increase his fear. He always was a nervous man. At first he startled me by his strange assertions, but now my fears are all dispelled.

Nel. Where is papa?

Mrs A. He has just gone down to his boat. He is going to leave us this afternoon.   (*places her arm around Nellie.*

Nel. Leave us! Where is he going?

Mrs A. On another voyage. He will not stay as long as usual this time. He will come and bid us good bye, before he starts.

Nel. O dear, I wish papa would never go on another voyage. I have not seen him half long enough. Let me go up to my room. Be sure and call me when papa comes.

Enter Larrie, R.

Mrs A. Yes, my daughter. (*exit Nellie,* R.—*Mrs. A. to Larrie*) Well, Larrie, where have you been?

Lar. O, I've been a lookin' arter things in gineral, an' makin' that bletherin', fiery, disdainful Biddy mind her business.

Mrs A. Why, what has she been doing?

Lar. Bin doin' enough, I should think. I'll tache the hateful, repugnant baste to affront me. She's the pest o' my life.

Mrs A. Why, what is the matter? What did she do?

Lar. Well, ye see, as I was about my usual ruteen o' business, I found it expadient to pass through the kitchen, an' as I chanced to look up, the provokin', scornful craitcher run her tongue out full length at me, just like that.   (*imitating.*

Mrs A. What did you do then?

Lar. I set down the pail I was carryin' and calmly surveyed her full in the face.

Mrs A. What did she do?

Lar. She puckered her little dirty face all up and repeated the same shameful act again.

Mrs A. I suppose you began to be a little angry by that time.

Lar. Wall—yes—ratherly.

Mrs A. Did she continue in this manner long?

Lar. Not a great while.

Mrs A. What did she do?

Lar. She didn't do very much. I took the matter into my own hands and she got set down in sech a way as she never was before.

Mrs A. Did you touch her before she did you?

Lar. D'ye s'pose I was goin' to wait for her to git the advantage? At first she got the start o' me, but I cautiously rached my hand around thus, (*imitating*) and sazed the leetle wad on the back of her head, then I set her down in the corner, an' I left her there bellerin', an' walked quietly away.

Enter Biddy, R. *crying.*

Mrs A. Here is Biddy now. Why Biddy! What have you and Larrie been doing?

Bid. That contemptible Irishman had the impudence to come to the place where I was at work, makin' faces an' givin' me all the sass his dirty tongue could utter, an'——

Lar. (*fiercely*) I never did sech a disgraceful thing.

Bid. You did.

Lar. I didn't.

Mrs A. (*interfering*) Not another word from either of you. Doubtless you are both to blame.

Together. { *Bid.* Yes, ye'll manage to take the part of that lawless upstart when——
Lar. Sure an' yer not layin' the blame on me when I was defendin'——

Mrs A. Stop! I've seen enough of these quarrels, and some means must be taken to prevent them. Both of you ought to be ashamed. Now go about your work, and don't let another complaint come to me from either of you.

Lar. (*goes to Biddy and puts his arm around her*) Come along, Biddy, we won't——

Bid. (*kicking*) Git out you infarnel dirty vagabond! Such impudence as that!

Lar. (*to Mrs. A.*) Jest see that! When I was about to make friends with her, she'd trate me like that!

Mrs A. Biddy, start for the kitchen! Don't let me have to speak to you again. (*Biddy and Larrie exit*, R.

Enter Harry, C. *a boy nine years old.*

Har. O dear! Where is Nellie? It's awful lonesome. I feel as if something terrible is going to happen.

Mrs A. Nellie is in her room, she will be down soon. What is the matter?

Har. I don't know. I feel uneasy and discontented.

Mrs A. Well, sit down and rest. When Mr. Alden comes, we will all go down to the dock with him and see him leave.

Har. Leave! Why, he isn't going away so soon, is he? I have not seen him long enough yet.

Mrs A. That's what Nellie said. But you see it is necessary for him to go. His voyage will be a short one this time, and when he returns, he will stay longer with us. You seem to be greatly attached to Mr. Alden.

Har. I am, and to you and Nellie, too. Why shouldn't I be? You took me from the street, a little ragged, dirty urchin, and gave me a chance to share with you in this bright and pleasant home. I feel as if I ought to call Mr. Alden, father, and you and Nellie, mother and sister. If anything should happen to separate us, O dear, what would I do?

Mrs A. (*aside*) I feel a greater interest in him than ever before. When I accidently met him in the street, I saw something in him that told me he was worthy of our attention and our home. I took him by the hand, led him to our door, clothed him, took the same care of him I would of my own child, and I believe I shall some day be rewarded for my care and watchfulness over him.

Enter Nellie, L.

Nel. Why, Harry, you here! I have been watching for you. I wondered where you were. But isn't it too bad papa is going to leave us so soon?

Har. Yes, and I am not at all pleased with it.

Enter Mr. Alden, c.

Mr A. My dear wife! I find it necessary to leave you immediately. The men had everything in readiness for starting much sooner than I expected, and we will clear as soon as I get back. Perhaps you and the children better walk down with me.

Mrs A. That is what we intended to do. After we see you leave, we shall take a long walk and make a few calls on our way home. (*Mrs. Alden, Nellie and Harry put on things*) The children manifest greater uneasiness at your departure now, than ever before.

Mr A. I am sorry! What if something should happen to prevent me from ever seeing them again!

Mrs A. It is not at all probable that anything unusual will occur.

Mr A. Perhaps I ought not to speak so. Remember what I told you. You cannot be too careful. Come on Nellie and Harry. (*all about to exit* c.

Enter Larrie, R.

Lar. Howld on a brafe moment. An' would you lave, Cap'n, without biddin' yer humble servant good bye?

Mr A. Pardon me, Larrie, I was so deep in thought that I forgot you. Take good care of Mrs. Alden and the children during my absence, and on my return I will reward you. Keep a sharp watch over everything.

Lar. Yes-sir-ee, that I will. Don't be alarmed about things when I'm around.

Mrs A. O, I forgot! Larrie, please call Biddy here just a moment.

Lar. Yes, mum, in a brafe moment.

Exit Larrie, R., *presently appears, Biddy with him.*

Mrs A. Biddy, while I am gone, you may bring a pail of water and wash the door casings. (*exit Mr. and Mrs. Alden, Harry and Nellie* c.

Bid. Yes mum. (*shakes her fist at them*) Jest let the first chance happen for me to heap my vingeance on that woman, an' wont I take advantage of it? Scroob the casings! Indade, it'll be a mighty dear scroob to her if I ken make it so.

Lar. Biddy, ye're the charm o' my life. I couldn't stay here without ye.

Bid. Well, I shall not stay here a great many days more to be insulted in this way. If anything is to be done it's left for Biddy to do. But Larrie is a gintleman—he ken set in the parlor an' intertain company. (*exit* R.

Lar. Bless the day when ye'll leave! I wonder what the Capt'n was thinkin' so earnestly about when he left. He tole me to take good care o' mistress an' children, while he was gone. He never tole me that afore. O, be gory, I see all through it! Faith an' I guess I'd better keep an eye on this hateful baste that jest went out. He'd noticed her odiousness. (*exit* c.

Enter Biddy, R., *with pail of water in one hand and a large towel saturated with water wadded up in the other. She catches her toe in the carpet and tumbles headlong on the floor. Larrie hearing the noise, enters, raises both hands in astonishment, and then bursts out into a hearty laugh.*

Bid. (*throwing the towel at Larrie*) Git out, ye dirty villain! Sneakin' 'round here. (*Larrie passes out* c., *just in time to escape the towel. Biddy writhes about pretending to be severely hurt*) Oh! that almost broke my back. There's a pain in my heart too; I shouldn't wonder if I broke it. I've heard of sech things as that. But then, Biddy ken do all the dirty work whether she's any back or heart either. (*goes to work*) I long for the time when I shall be out o' this.

Enter Harold, L.

Bid. (*thinking it is Larrie, jumps down from the chair on which she is standing, and about to throw the towel at him*) Beg your dear pardon, sir, I thought 'twas that provokin' bogtrotter.

Harold. Excuse me for appearing so abruptly. I have a proposition to make to you.

Bid. (*carelessly dropping the towel*) A propisition! Sure an I've been expectin', a long time, some one would propose to me. I knew I didn't possess all this beauty for nothing. Strange ye've not did this before.

Harold. Well, you see I've had no good opportunity. I desired to see you when the folks were away. Can you keep a secret for me?

Bid. To be sure I can, sir. It's just as much for my advantage as yours to keep it a secret. Why, sir, I'm only nineteen now, an' do you belave I ought to waste my swateness here, in slavery to these overbearin' people?

Harold. Surely you ought not to. You don't speak of these folks as if they were your special favorites.

Bid. Indade, sir, they're not. All the dirty work is tucked onto me jest because I'm always willin' to do it. I was afther remarkin' a short time ago, that I should be glad when I was out o' this.

Harold. You don't like the mistress very well, then?

Bid. No. Go on with yer proposin', I'm anxious to hear.

Harold. (*aside*) She seems to misconstrue what I say, but I think I can trust her. (*aloud*) Well, this woman you are living with, was once a beautiful, charming creature.

Bid. Jest like myself!

Harold. For a long time I paid my attentions to her, but she refused my offer of marriage, and——

Bid. Aint ye glad of it since ye set yer eyes on me?

Harold. Every since she rejected me, I have vowed to make her repent of her conduct, and I think the time is at hand. Her husband is about to depart on another voyage. This will make it easier for me to bring about what I desire. The plan I have in view is this: I intend to rob the Alden's of their daughter. I want your assistance in this. I will liberally reward you for it, and if you desire a better situation, I will procure it for you. Will you lend me your aid?

Bid. (*covering her face with her hands*) Pardon me, sir, I thought 'twas the other thing you was going to propose. Sure an, I'll be afther givin' ye all the help desired. I've been wantin' a chance to cover that woman with my hate, an' now I've the opportunity.

Harold. That is capital. (*aside*) All my plans are working to perfection. (*aloud*) Now, as to the way in which we shall do this. Sometime when Mrs. Alden is going out, you manage to have the child left with you. I shall pass frequently, and when the opportunity comes, you signal me and I will come and take her. Take great interest in her before her mother, but be careful not to over do it so as to create suspicion. I must leave, for Mrs. Alden will soon return, and then my plans will be liable to be overturned. It will not be at all difficult to gain possession of her, for I shall make her presents, from time to time, to gain her favor. Mind you keep this to yourself.

Bid. Sure an' I'll kape it as sacret as a mice under a haystack. An' wouldn't ye like to take the boy too?

Harold. Yes, I'll take them both. I have an out-of-the-way place, four hundred miles down the coast, where I can place them out of reach of any one. (*exit* L.

Bid. (*goes to work briskly*) I'll see whether I'm to be kept here for a nagur waiter or not. I'm so happy I could sing. (*sings.*

> That night on the road as I went to Darbee,
> A terrible craitcher set up in a tree;
> In a tree that grew out o' the side o' a hill,
> And the craitcher cried out whippowill, whippowill.

Enter Larrie, R.

Lar. What ye singin' so swately about, Biddy? Ye're mighty happy all at once, seems to me. Ye've changed yer tune since I see ye last.

Bid. (*fiercely*) I'll change your tune, if ye don't mind yer business.

Lar. Change my tune! Ye tried that once in the kitchen, didn't ye? D'ye recollect with what aise I planted ye down in the corner?

Bid. Well, I reckon ye wont do it again! Ye lawless upstart, ye wont have a chance to pick on me in this way a great many times more. I'm goin' to stan' up for my rights now. Ye know the mistress allays favors ye.

Lar. (*he has been regarding her with astonishment*) O-ho-ho-ho! Ye've sang that melody iver since I knew ye. O, Biddy, ye'll niver swally any one alive.

Bid. Sure an' I'll not swally your rotten carcass, I ken tell ye that. The first chance I git, I'm goin' to have me a hoosband, then we'll see who'll come off boss.

Lar. A hoosband! Who in creation will it be?

Bid. When he gits his fist into yer nose once, he'll make ye think of Ould Ireland.

Lar. O, it's a big Irishman then. I guess ye won't be sharp enough to catch a son of Emerald Isle very soon. What's the matter o' ye? Have ye had a call while I've been gone?

Bid. Wouldn't ye like to know?

Lar. I don't care whether or whether.

Bid. Well, I guess ye'd have to wait till ye'd find out, if ye did care.

Lar. O, but I'll tell the mistress, when she comes. That'll fetch ye 'round as quick as anything. Here she comes now.

Enter Mrs. Alden, Nellie and Harry, c.

Mrs A. What's the trouble now?

Lar. Biddy has been afther havin' a call while I was gone, and refused to tell who it was.

Bid. That hateful bogtrotter has been tryin' to provoke me again, with his infarnel slander, and——

Mrs A. Stop! Now, Larrie, I'll hear what you have to say.

Bid. (*fiercely*) Yes, ye'll always manage to give him the priference, an' belave all his lies, ye hateful ould croaking jade.

Mrs A. Biddy, pack up your things quickly, and leave! Don't you dare stay here another moment.

Bid. (*kneels before Mrs. A. with clasped hands*) O, but if you'll only forgive me this time, I'll promise niver more to offend ye.

Mrs A. This is not the first time. You don't seem to realize how great an offence you have been guilty of.

Bid. O, I can see my fault now. I niver beheld it so before.

Mrs A. Well, as you seem to manifest so great penitence, I don't know but I will try you once more.

Bid. Belave me, it will niver happen again.   (*exit Larrie, c.*

Mrs A. Now, Biddy, you may leave this work as soon as you finish it, and prepare dinner.

Bid. Why, I've it finished now.

Mrs A. Very well, I'll excuse you then. (*exit Biddy R., leaving pail*) Now children, you must not go out in the street unless some of us are with you. You had better sit down here and rest yourselves till after dinner.

Nel. Why, mother, do you tell us not to go on the street alone?

Mrs A. Because your father was very anxious that I should guard you carefully, lest some accident should happen to you.

Nel. I don't see how anything is going to harm us now, more than ever before.

Har. You cannot always tell what is going to happen.

Nel. Why, Harry, what do you mean by saying that?

Har. O, never mind! It is not at all likely that anything bad is going to happen.

Mrs A. I hope not. Your father loves you so, he is always careful to keep you out of harm's way.

Har. I think we have better reason to hope he will meet with no disaster, than he has to worry about us.

Mrs A. That is so, Harry, and if he returns safe, I shall be very thankful. O, dear! what if he should be wrecked on some unfriendly island!

Nel. Now, mother, don't speak so! He is not going to be wrecked.

Mrs A. We will hope for the best, and wait patiently for his safe return. Let us go up stairs and watch his boat till out of sight. (*about to exit* L.)

Enter Biddy, R.

Bid. I forgot my pail, so I thought I'd come and git it. O, but what a kind missus ye are, and I love yer children so, too. (*embraces and kisses Nellie, who tries to resist her*) Sure, an' what for ye try to push me away? I always took a magnificent interest in ye. Strange ye'd do this!

Mrs A. Nellie is not feeling well to-day.

Bid. The poor little thing! How I love her. (*hugs Nellie again.*) She must have a dose of Wizard Ile.

Mrs A. (*aside*) What can that woman mean by acting so lovingly towards Nellie. By the way, I guess it was well I showed my authority when I did. (*To children*) Children, you may wait here a little while till I come back. I forgot that I had an engagement with Mrs. Smith. (*exit* R.

Bid. (*aside*) Here is a capital chance, if the gentleman is only at hand. (*looks out* C.) I hope he'll come along. It won't do to miss this chance, if I can see that man. (*children about to go off* L.) Hold on, ye little dears. An' would ye try to avoid yer best friend?

Nel. We are going up stairs to watch papa's boat. He is nearly out of sight now.

Bid. The boat! Sure an' that's out o' sight long ago. I noticed that, when I was in the kitchen. Jest ye set down here now, whilst I sing ye one of owld Erins swate tunes. Ye didn't know I was a singer, did ye?

Nel. } Why, no! can you sing?
Har. }

Bid. Ho-o-o-o, to be sure I ken! Ye don't know what a desperate voice I'm the possesser of! An' did ye iver go to the museum?

Nel. } Never.
Har. }

Bid. Well, I've been there. I'll sing ye what I saw there. (*sings.*

There were mad-cats, and geese, and a five legged cow,
Mad-dogs, and wild hogs, and a thing like a crow;
One side stood a black snake, a wolf, and a bear,
And behind stood a thing like McFliggen's owld mare.

Enter Harold, C.

Bid. (*turns hastily around*) Who's the impudence to interrupt me whin —O, I beg your pardon, sir! I was jest amusing the children in accordance with yer instructions, as—— (*Harold motions her to stop talking.*)

Harold. I called to take the children out to ride.

Har. We don't want to ride. (*children about to exit* R.

Harold. Hold on, children, your mother wants you to go and ride with me. I just saw her on the street, and she told me to come and take you out to enjoy the refreshing breeze outside. Come on; I'm sure you will like the ride. Get ready. (*they do so.*

Bid. (*to Harold*) Would ye let me ride with ye down town jest a leetle ways, to get some bafe for dinner? I'm so tired.

Harold. Certainly. Hurry up, all of you and get ready. (*exit Biddy* R.

Har. What are you in a hurry about?

Harold. O, we must get out as soon as possible, so as to take the benefit of the delightful breeze.

Enter Biddy, R., *dressed in an old red shawl and hood.*

Bid. Don't I look capital in this rig? Folks won't know but its your wife, I look so becomin'.

Harold. Come on, let's be going. (*takes Nellie by one hand Harry by the other—they are reluctant to go*) what are you hanging back for? Come along. (*all exit, c., a pause.*

Enter Larrie, R.

Lar. I wonder where all the folks have gone? I can't find any one about the house, not even Biddy. She'd better be hurrying up that dinner, for I'm getting rather hungry. (*a song or dance may be introduced, after which Larrie goes out c.*

Enter Mrs. Alden, L.

Mrs A. Well, children— (*surprised*) Why, I left them here a short time ago. O, I guess they have gone up stairs to watch the boat. I'll go to the kitchen, and see how near dinner is ready. (*exit R., but shortly returns, alarmed*) Why, Biddy is gone, the fire all out, and no dinner! What does this mean? Where can she be? and the children! I'll go and look for them. (*exit R.*

Enter Larrie, c.

Lar. (*excited*) Where's the missus? The man told me he saw Biddy and the children, riding with a black whiskered man. I shouldn't wonder if that dirty, contemptable Biddy was up to something she'd no business to be.

Enter Mrs. Alden, R.

Lar. And what for you let the children and Biddy ride with the man with black whiskers?

Mrs A. (*frightened*) Biddy and the children riding with whom?

Lar. They're riding at full speed, and are now out o' sight, with the black whiskered man that passes so often.

Mrs A. What did my husband tell me? Run and send some one after them, quick! (*exit Larrie, c.*) My Nellie and Harry! O, dear! My children riding with Harold, and already out of sight! Why couldn't I have foreseen it? I see now what Biddy's affection meant. I see what the orange meant! Oh dear, O dear, why didn't I dismiss her when I attempted to. My husband out of sight, and my children stolen; and warned before hand. What shall I do, what shall I do I (*faints, and falls on floor.*

Enter Larrie, c.

Lar. The police say—What! Dead!

Hastily starts to go out, and returns, goes out c., but immediately returns, excited and confused, and dodges about the stage.

CURTAIN.

ACT II.

SCENE FIRST.—*Zeke Crowell's house, four hundred miles down the coast. Doors R. and L., window c. Table c., at which Mrs. Crowell, Harry and Nellie, dressed in rags, are sitting, having just finished supper. Trap door near R.*

Mrs C. (*rising from table, wiping her mouth with apron*) Well, children, you may get up now and clear off the table and wash the dishes, for I guess yer father won't be in till late, and——

Har. What do you want to call him our father for? He is no relation to us, and you know it. I would be ashamed to call him father, and so would Nellie.

Mrs C. (*lighting her pipe*) Ashamed to call him father! Wall, ye ought to be mighty glad to call him father. Ye orter think yourselves well off here. Ye have enough tew eat and keep warm, and hev a place tew sleep under shingles. When I wuz a gal, I should thought myself well off if I could had as much as that.

Har. If you could see what we had before we were brought to this lonesome place, you wouldn't think it strange that we want to get away from here, and we intend to some time, too.

Mrs C. Wall, I guess ye won't do anything very wonderful while Zeke Crowell has charge of ye. I've heerd little foolish boys talk before. I never seed a young one brought up in the city yit that knew anything. City folks don't know nothin' themselves, and so their young one's can't know nothin'. I'm mighty glad, I wasn't brought up among the fools. They don't seem to realize that they spile their young ones. I don't suppose that your folks knew it when they spilt you.

Nel. Well, I guess we are not so near "spilt" as you think we are. You are so ignorant, you are not capable of judging.

Mrs C. (*excited*) Do you tell me I don't know nothin'? Ef I had a gad here, I'd wallop you. (*shakes her*) You're another city-brought-up gal. It's jest as I told ye a minit ago—that city folks don't know nothin'. They jest go and pay out all their money for their children, and make fools ou 'em. Sech a dress as you had on when you come here. It looked jest as if some one had wadded up the cloth and throwed it at ye. I stripped that up mighty quick and put it in the carpet rags. I suppose ye had one o' them ere things ye drum down on, when ye was to home didn't ye?

Nel. Yes, I had a fine piano.   (*bursts out crying.*)

Mrs C. A pi-an-ny! I should think as much! I wouldn't hev one of 'em in my house a great while, before 'twould git split up for kindling wood. Now go at them dishes and wash 'em up, and stop that bellerin'.

(*Mrs. Crowell sits. Children go to work at dishes—Nellie crying.*)

Nel. O, dear, Harry, what did we ever go with that man for? I wonder where mother is.

Har. Don't cry, Nellie, all will yet be well.

Nel. O, if father only knew where we are! we wouldn't be obliged to stay here a great while.

Har. Well, he is not going to be gone a great while, you know. He will find out where we are, and come and rescue us.

Enter Zeke Crowell, L., *with a large bottle under one arm, and a broken jar containing a small package, under the other.*

Zeke. What's that ye're talkin' about, young man? Who's comin' arter ye?

Mrs C. They've been talkin' about going away, and all this sort of thing, and I tell 'em——

Zeke. Never mind what you told 'em. As soon as I git rested and take a little grog, so I feel like it, I'll try and persuade the young man to stay here awhile. Old woman, you might go arter that gad, so as to have it ready.

Exit Mrs. C. L., but presently returns with a large whip.

Har. I don't care how much you whip me, if you don't whip Nellie. We don't belong here, anyhow, and we want to go home.

Zeke. (*setting the bottle on the mantle, and the jar on table, so that Mrs. Crowell sees the break*) Want to get away, do ye? I'll try and change yer mind on that.   (*seizes whip and about to strike Harry.*)

Mrs C. (*seeing her jar broken, breaks in fiercely*) Zeke Crowell, ye've broke my best butter jar, and I'm almost a mind to throw it right straight at yer old head. It's one I've had every since I was married.

Zeke. Wall, ye jest throw it at my head if ye dare. I feel jest good-na-tured enough to hev a row with an old fool of a woman. I'll lay the gad 'round these ere youngones till they can't stand up, and then I'll mall it over you till there ain't a bit left of it.

Mrs C. Zeke Crowell, if you ever strike me a blow, I'll have you arrest-ed before the day is out, I ken tell ye that, now. I might as well send a boy three years old to market, as to send you. How did ye break that jar?

Zeke. None o' yer business, ye old jade.

Mrs C. Wall, I never see the beat o' you. What did ye git for the eggs?

Zeke. I got a muddy coat for 'em. I stumbled into the gutter and spilt-ed 'em.

Mrs C. (*enraged*) Zeke Crowell, I've a good mind to jest strike ye over the head with the tongs. A man that don't know more that, orter be learn-ed sunthin'. Here I do all the work, and set the hens, and gather the eggs, and then to hev you go and cut up such a caper as this. I never in all my life see the beat of it.

Zeke. (*goes to the bottle and drinks*) I'll give nature a jog, and then we'll see if I can keep pace with the old woman.

(*Nellie, who has been washing dishes, drops a plate, breaking it.*)

Mrs C. There, I never! Another one of my best dishes broke.

Zeke. (*takes whip, seizes Nellie by the arm*) I feel in jest good spirits enough to give you a rawhiding.

Har. (*entreating*) Please don't whip Nellie. If you are going to whip anybody, whip me.

Zeke. (*seizing Harry*) I'll lick ye both. Come on here.

(*they exit* L. *Blows of whip, and cries of the children are heard.*)

Mrs C. Zeke, Zeke! don't strike 'em too hard.

Zeke. (*outside*) Shet up yer head, ye old fool, or I'll whale you too.

Mrs C. That man never has any mercy when he once gits to lickin' a youngone. He tried that game on me once, but I worsted him. He never has dared touch me since.

Enter Zeke, L., *with the children, crying.*

Zeke. Now both of ye go off to bed, and don't let me hear another word from ye to-night. (*exit children,* R.)

Mrs C. O, I forgot! Zeke, did ye git the newspaper? (*Zeke does not answer her*) I say, Zeke! did ye git the newspaper? (*pause*) Zeke!

Zeke. What!

Mrs C. I asked ye if ye got the paper?

Zeke. Yes, I got the paper.

Mrs C. Let me have it, I want to read.

Zeke. (*throws paper in her face*) There! take it if ye want it. (*they both light their pipes. Mrs. Crowell puts on glasses and goes to reading*) I tell ye what, old woman, I'm going to git rid of them ere young ones jest as quick as I ken. If I can't git rid of 'em any other way, I'll hang stones to their necks and sink 'em. I won't have 'em round here a great while longer.

Mrs C. Why, Zeke! they'd hang ye if ye done that.

Zeke. I don't care what they'd do. Them ere young ones will have to leave here before to-morrow night. Mark my word for that. They don't know nothin', and ye might as well try to learn a block of wood somethin' as to try to learn 'em. Who wants sech critters as that around. I don't, and I ain't goin' to neither.

Mrs C. Well, Zeke, you and I agree on one thing esackly. That's about these ere children not knowin' nothin'. I jest expressed my 'pinion on that before you come. I'm mighty glad I never was brought up, the way they've been. You never would have had me, if I'd been brought up the way they have been, would ye?

Zeke. No, I don't s'pose I would. I got a poor enough bargain as it was. I come mighty near not havin' ye; and I guess I'd been better off, if I'd left ye after I promised to have ye.

Mrs C. Wall I declare! Zeke Crowell, you ken leave now, if ye want tew. Ye spoke about gittin' rid of them children. How ye goin' to do it?

Zeke. O, ye're mighty willin' to change the subject, when I tell ye too much truth, ain't ye I

Mrs C. How ye goin' to manage with 'em?

Zeke. Well now, old woman, if anybody asks ye, you tell 'em ye don't know. *(takes off his overcoat, throws it over her head.*

Mrs C. *(throws it off, excited)* Zeke Crowell, I won't stay here another minit to be insulted in this way. *(exit Mrs. Crowell through trap door.*

Zeke. Good riddance. I ain't one of the kind to have an old woman bossin me 'round.—Let's see. How's the best way to dispose of them ere young ones? I guess I'll git 'em up now, and take 'em to the beach, tie a stone to their necks, and sink 'em. Nobody will ever know it, and it ain't at all likely that chap will ever come arter 'em, that brought 'em here. *(hesitates)* Yes, I guess that's the best way. *(exit R., and presently returns leading Harry and Nellie)* Come on here; we'll take a little walk down to the beach.

Har. What are you going to the beach for, this time of night?

Zeke. Now see here, young man, don't ask me any questions. It's my business why I'm a goin' to the beach. Perhaps it's to give you a bath.

Nel. O, dear! I don't want to go. Please don't take us off down there.

Zeke. *(attempting to lead them off L., both resisting)* We'll see whether you'll go or not. *(both pull away from him. He chases them around stoge.*

Enter Harold, L.

Harold. Hallo, Zeke! What's up now? Won't they mind you?

Nel. O, dear! What can we do? That awful man here again.

Harold. *(advancing)* Come right here to me, both of you. *(children about to exit R. Harold seizes them)* Hold on! Strange, you'd try to escape me. *(to Zeke)* But I say, Zeke, what was the trouble when I came in?

Zeke. *(regarding Harold with astonishment)* Well now, seems to me ye're takin' considerable liberty in my house. Who's gi'n ye leave to come in, in this way? Ye didn't know I was boss of this shanty, did ye?

Harold. Never mind. That's all right. You see I'm mighty careful of these youngsters; I wouldn't lose one of them for a fortune. I have an object in view. I knew when I left them with you, they would be perfectly secure; but I concluded to change their place of residence, if you are willing.

Zeke. Willin', of course I'm willin'! That's jest what I want ye to do. I didn't s'pose you'd ever be 'round arter 'em again.

Harold. Well, I concluded to send them farther away from here, for I didn't know but what some one might run across them accidently, and be the means of handing them over to their mother; and that I don't intend shall be done. I have a friend who is about to start for the South Pacific, and he has agreed te take them with him. *(both children scream, and attempt to get away)* No, I guess I wouldn't try that. You are not very well acquainted with me yet.

Enter Mrs. Crowell, through trap door.

Mrs C. Land sakes alive! Zeke Crowell, what on airth—*(sees Harold—raises both hands in astonishment)* Who's that?

Zeke. Wall there, old woman, you've got taken back once in yer life, I hope. This 'ere man has come arter the young ones, and he's a goin' to take 'em too. You needn't set up your blarney about it neither.

Nel. O. if father could only step in, and rescue us now!

Harold. Your father never will see you again. His ship encountered a storm, and was wrecked. All went to the bottom with him. So you have no hope of him.

Nel. What will happen to us next? Father shipwrecked, and drowned. All hope is now gone, Harry.

Har. Don't believe what this man says. He lied to us once, and he will do it again. We cannot rely on what he says.

Harold. Young man, do you tell me I lie? Don't do that again, sir.

Mrs C. Then ye're goin' to take 'em away, be ye?

Harold. Yes, I must take them away.

Mrs C. I kinder hate to have 'em leave now, they've been here quite a spell.

Zeke. Hate to have 'em leave! That's as much as a foolish old woman knows. I should think we'd had enough trouble over these 'ere brats for nothin'. I'm mighty glad to git rid on 'em.

Mrs C. (*to Harold*) Where do ye think o' takin' on 'em?

Zeke. Now, old woman, it don't make any difference to you where he's goin' to take 'em He's a goin' to take 'em away from here, and that's enough for you to know.

Mrs C. I didn't ask you, Zeke Crowell.

Zeke. No, I know ye didn't; but I answered ye, so it's jest as well. You're jest like any other old woman, comin' here, and stickin' yer nose into what's none o' yer business.

Mrs C. Zeke Crowell, I'll give ye to understand that I've got as good a right here as you have.

Zeke. Yes, got a better right, ain't ye?

Harold. (*going* L.) Come on here, young folks, I guess we'll have to be tramping.

Mrs C. Goodness me! ye ain't goin' to take them off, sech a cold night as this, without nothin' 'round 'em be ye? Hold on! Let me git somethin' to put on 'em.

Harold. They don't need anything. I'll risk 'em. I've got an old blanket I can roll 'em up in. Good night. (*exit with the children,* L.)

Zeke. There, I've got that job off my mind. Now I'll go to my bunk and see if I can get a little rest.

Mrs C. Where did he say he was goin' with 'em?

Zeke. (*taking a drink from bottle*) Don't ask me any more questions to-night.

Mrs C. (*walking spitefully away*) O, if you ain't the meanest man. (*exit through trap door.*)

Zeke. 'Twas mighty fortunate that that man come just when he did, or 'twould been a goner for them young ones. I told the old woman they'd have to leave here before to-morrow night. (*exit through trap door.*)

The lights are somewhat darkened. Larrie takes out the window c. and stands outside looking in.

Lar. Indade! I'm sure this must be the place. I guess they're all to bed before this time o' night. I'll venture in, and see what I can find. (*He jumps upon the window sill, lantern in hand, listens a moment, then jumps down inside. He walks slowly, listening at every step*) It looks as if they might be a rough crowd here. I'd better be afther lookin' out for myself I guess. (*taking a book from the mantle*) A book! be me soul! P'raps I can find out somethin' in it, about the children. Let's see if there's a name. (*turns book around several times, looks at name*) Some kind of awkward scrawling, I can't make it out. I never did learn to read that kind of letters, except my own name. (*sees Zeke's bottle*) I wonder what's in that? (*takes out cork and smells*) O, be gary! Some o' the craitcher surely. (*laughs*) I've been wanting to get some o' that, this good while. (*takes a drink*) That's good. I wish my throat was a mile long, so I could taste it a long time. That'll put new life into my limbs, and mettle into my heels. It's rather fortunate I stopped here. (*about to take another drink, but hears a noise*) Hark! what's that? They're gettin' wind of my presence here.

Sees Zeke coming up through the trap door. Drops the bottle, breaking it, and tumbles hastily out over the window sill. Stands outside looking in.

Zeke. The old woman must conjure up something to git me up, lookin' round. I don't believe she heard anything: She must have it that the old cat was in the cupboard, or somewhere else.

Lar. (*aside*) I'm sure, sir, 'twas somewhere else. At least I saw him on the mantel a minit ago.

Zeke. (*sees bottle broken*) What! How come this to be done? I guess the old woman was right about the cat bein' here.

Lar. (*aside*) I'm sure she was.

Zeke. The bottle broke, and my grog all spilled.

Lar. (*aside*) Yes, some of it spilled down my throat. I'm rather sorry it's broke, too, for I wanted another dose of it myself.

Zeke. If I can find that 'ere cat, there'll be one less of that kind of animals 'round here. (*looks around the room.*)

Lar. (*aside*) I'm sure, sir, you'll find no cat to-night.

Zeke. I don't see nothin' of it.

Lar. (*aside*) You're blind, then.

Zeke. (*raising his hand*) I thought I felt a gust of wind then.

(*starts towards the window..*)

Lar. To the divil with yer wind. Ye won't be sharp enough to find this cat. (*laughs, and replaces window.*)

Zeke. (*looking at window*) I don't see nothin' wrong, except my bottle. I'll go back to bed, and to-morrow morning that cat will have to die.

(*exit down trap door.*)

Lar. (*takes out window and cautiously enters*) I'll take one more look so as to be sure, and then I'll lave. It wont do for me to go out over that window-sill, so hastily many times; it hurt my back. I've always been a little lame every since I fell from that ninth story tenement. (*goes to trap door, looks down*) I think they must sleep in the cellar here. I don't believe I'll venture down there. I'll just shut down the door and plant the table on it, and then I can look around as long as I please. (*closes door, places table over it*) Now I'll be afther makin' a search. (*as he starts away the door is raised by Zeke, overturning the table. Larrie rushes out through window, leaving his lantern behind*) O, be gorry! I've left my lantern. (*jumps in, seizes lantern, and passes out closely followed by Zeke with an old musket. Mrs. Crowell stands with both hands raised in astonishment.*)

QUICK CURTAIN.

☞ There is supposed to be a lapse of twenty years, between the second and third acts. A suitable change must be made for the characters.

ACT III.

SCENE FIRST.—*Mrs. Alden's tenement. Doors* R. L. *and* C. *Stove* L. *of* C. *Table* R.

Enter Mrs. Alden C., *dressed in rags, carrying a basket of potatoes on one arm, and a basket of chips on the other.*

Mrs A. (*setting down the baskets*) O, dear! when will the end come? How much longer will I be compelled to drag out this miserable existence! I could better endure such a life as this, if it had never been mine to possess wealth and influence. But now, this hard life is made a thousand times harder to me, since it recalls to me the once beautiful home in the city, and more than all, the contented and happy family of which I was a member. But alas! all this has vanished. My husband's ship wrecked, he cast adrift and lost, and my beautiful children stolen. Oh, how can I bear such thoughts as these! Why! it's just twenty years ago to-day since we were separated for the last time. Yes, just twenty years. During all this time I have waited patiently, for some revelation of fate. O, if I could once more see my children—all hope of my husband is now gone. They were nine years old when stolen. Twenty years ago. Is it possible that they are now, if living, twenty-nine years old? I wonder how they would look. I can imagine Harry's manly countenance, and Nellie's womanly dignity. What have they suffered since last I saw them? But why do I indulge such thoughts as these? they can never be restored to me, no never. That villain, who has made me wretched, is too artful to be brought to justice. That is what my husband once told me—If I had only heeded it. He has robbed me of my family and my property, and if he can ascertain my whereabouts, he will exert himself to make me more miserable. O, merciful heaven! what next lies in store for me? Take me from this misery, for I cannot endure it?

    (*bursts into tears—takes up basket of potatoes and begins to peal them.*

    The c. door gently opens, and Harold enters unobserved by Mrs. Alden.

Harold. I hope I have found you at last.

Mrs A. (*screams, drops the basket, and starts back*) Who is it?

Harold. Me.

Mrs A. (*aside*) Harold! that villain, come to torment me again. I was thinking myself secure in this place. Let me die rather than be the subject of his torture.

Harold. I have come to make a proposal to you by which you can profit.

Mrs A. What! Restore my children?

Harold. No, you can never again see them; they both perished in a foreign land.

Mrs A. Leave me to die. I have seen enough of this world.

Harold. You can yet be made happy.

Mrs A. How?

Harold. By a marriage with me. Will you accept my offer?

Mrs A. Never! Leave the house you wretch. Sooner than join myself to you, I'll drink the cup of misfortune to the very dregs.

Harold. That I intended you should do, from the first. When you had suffered to such an extent, that I thought myself fully satisfied, then I intended to offer you my hand and protection. Your husband no longer lives. You can relieve yourself of this wretchedness only by a union with me. You can be made happy by this alone.

Mrs A. Happy! What affection can I have for a man, who has taken from me all that made life dear; who has caused twenty years of the bitterest grief? Such happiness would be misery, a thousand times greater than that which I now bear.

Harold. You refuse at your peril.

Mrs A. I refuse.

Harold. Very well. I'll give you time to reflect; I shall soon return. If your decision then remains unchanged, something much more severe than you have ever experienced, lies in wait for you. Consider well.

    (*exit c.*

Mrs A. What shall I do? accept his offer, or resign myself to his torture? I would sooner die than live with such a man. Tired of life, wearried with everything; why should I desire to live? But I can never accept his proposal; for I should be more miserable then even than I am now. Something tells me to reject all his advances. If he could only be detected and brought to justice! but no, he is too shrewd for that. He will soon return, and finding my decision unchanged, he will renew his cruelty. (*hesitates*) I will flee from this place, and attempt to find another more concealed from Harold. I have nothing to carry except my poor torn clothes, these can soon be collected, and then I will depart. I must make haste, for it is uncertain when he will return. (*puts on bonnet and shawl, about to exit c. Hearing a loud knock, she hastily takes off bonnet and shawl*) There, that is Harold, now! I ought to have been quicker. O, dear! what shall I do? —And yet, he would not knock, would he?

Enter. Nellie, c., exhausted and with the appearance of having been in the water.

Nel. Please may I take shelter under your roof a short time ? Our boat struck a rock, a short distance from the shore, and was dashed to pieces, nearly all the passengers were lost; scarcely half a dozen will be saved. I, myself lost consciousness twice while floating on a piece of wreck, but I was so fortunate as to reach the shore in safety at last. This house being the only one in sight, I endeavored to reach it as soon as possible.

Mrs A. (*aside*) It is not Harold disguised in female clothing to deceive me is it ? I hardly know how to take things, since he commenced his cruelty, I doubt everything lately. Perhaps he is employing some one to raise my expectations, and then suddenly break me down again ; he knows the shock it would occasion would nearly kill me, and that is what he wants. I'll venture to ask her name, at least; and the port for which she is bound. (*to Nellie*) O, dear ! I cannot bear to think of shipwreck. For what port are you bound ?

Nel. For Philadelphia.

Mrs A. That is where I used to live. What is your name ?

Nel. Well, my name was changed when I was very young, in order to make me forget it, but I remember it well; it was Nellie Alden. I was stolen from home twenty years ago, but I am now free, and in search of my parents.

Mrs A. (*aside and excited*) An imposition from Harold surely ! (*to Nellie*) Leave me instantly ! It is not at all unexpected ! Harold sent you here. You are not my child, she perished years ago.

Nel. But why do you speak of Harold ? has he made you miserable too ? Harold was the man that took me from home.

Mrs A. (*aside*) If she is not my child, perhaps I can get her sympathy, even if sent here by Harold.

Nel. (*greatly interested*) Speak, for I desire to know your story ! Pray, what is your name ?

Mrs A. My name is Laura Alden. (*Nellie all excitement*) Harold has deprived me of everything—my family, my property, all. Both children perished in a foreign country. I received this intelligence a short time ago from Harold himself. It is impossible for you to be my child, for she is dead.

Nel. (*aside*) Is she my mother, and in this condition ? She spoke of her children; if she means Harry, I am sure it is she. I'll ask her. (*to Mrs. Alden*) You speak of your children. Who were the others beside your daughter ?

Mrs A. He was not my own child ; his name was Harry Mansfield.

Nel. (*rushes to her mother and embraces her*) My dear, dear, mother ! I am your lost child. I did not perish, as Harold intended. Kind fortune has watched over me during this long, long time. I came very near being lost when so near you, but even now, the rock on which our ship struck, is fortunate for me, else perhaps, I could have never found you.

Mrs A. (*aside*) It is truly Nellie ! How strange ! (*to Nellie*) My child, my child ! can it be that you have been preserved and restored to me ? I never expected to see you again. In a moment more, I should not have met you ; for I was about to flee, in order to avoid Harold. I have met misfortune upon misfortune since I lost you, and this has been made greater on account of my anxiety for you. You are not deceiving me, are you ? You are sure your name is Nellie Alden ?

Nel. Yes, I am truly your daughter.

Mrs A. Ah, yes ! I can see your old looks now.

Nel. Harry was on board too.

Mrs A. Harry ! Where is he ? He was not drowned, was he ?

Nel. No. I left him on the beach, assisting others who were less fortunate than ourselves.

Mrs A. He lives then ?

Nel. Yes, and I must hasten and find him.

Mrs A. I will go with you. We will find him and come back here, for Harold will shortly return to torment me; but Harry will protect me, I know he will. Let us hasten. I thought it was Harold when I first heard you.   *(both about to exit, c.*

Enter Mr. Alden and Harry, c.

Nel. Why, Harry! have you come? We were just going to find you. You do not know whom I have met here in this desolate region.

Har. It is not unexpected to you, perhaps, whom I have met and recognized. You remember our conversation about the man on board, who looked as your father used to.

Nel. Yes, I remember, and——

Har. He is your father.

Mrs A. Merciful heaven! my husband, and alive!

Nel. Harry, I have found mother, here she is.

Mr A. My wife and child! At last, at last! Fortune has smiled on me at last.   *(takes Nellie by the hand, at the same time embraces Mrs. Alden.*

Nel. My dear father.

Mrs A. My husband! my boy! *(takes. Harry by the hand)* I thought you all had perished. Great is the misery I have endured since I last saw you. Great must have been yours too. This is indeed a strange meeting. It is just twenty years ago to-day since our last meeting. Strange, strange, that we should be brought together again at this time. Only to-night I was lamenting my fate, and wishing myself dead. But for the first time in twenty years has my grief been turned to joy. I can hardly believe my own eyes. My dear husband! I supposed you perished on that last voyage.

Mr A. True, my ship was wrecked, and I was the only one who survived. I floated for two whole days, on a fragment of the wreck, without food, and without sufficient clothing. I was finally born to a hostile shore, where I was compelled to serve as a slave to the unfriendly and barbarous natives; subjected to all manner of indignities, until an opportunity presented itself for me to escape, which I took advantage of, and which was the means of restoring me to my family. No one rejoices more at this meeting than myself.

Har. Long would be the story Nellie and I could relate of our unhappiness, since we were taken from home by that base wretch, Harold. I wonder if he still lives. If he does——

Mr A. Harold! ah, I see! it was a mystery to me, why I should meet you and Nellie here; you were stolen from home by Harold; but if——

Mrs A. Hush! Harold called a short time ago, and offered me his hand in marriage. I refused. He departed, but will soon return, to ascertain if my decision remains the same. He has robbed me of my home, and he has taken advantage of everything in his power to make me miserable. Let us make a surprise party for him.

Har. Harold will soon return! let us give him a warm reception. Mother, you stay here, and await his coming. Father, Nellie and I will retire, and when Harold has proceeded far enough with his cruelty, we will interfere and surprise him. I hope that infernal Biddy will come with him.

Mrs. A. It is not at all likely that Biddy will come with him. Perhaps you had better withdraw, for it is time for him to return.

Har. Come on let us prepare ourselves for Harold.

(exit Harry, Nellie and Mr. Alden, L.

Mrs. A. I did not suppose when Harold left, that I should be able to receive him in this way. He supposes my family dead, and that he has full sway over everything. Sadly disappointed he will be! I can now meet him with joy instead of sorrow. How glad I am that I had not gone when Nellie came. Here comes Harold now.

Enter Harold and Biddy, c.

Mrs A. *(aside)* I declare! Biddy is with him. Harry's wish will be gratified.

Bid. O, this is the place where the hateful owld craitcher lives, is it? Be my sowl! that's her surely. (*advancing towards Mrs. Alden*) How d'ye do ye owld croakin' jade! Ye're cuttin' a different swell from what ye was once, ain't ye? Let's hear if yer voice is so commandin' as it used to be! Spake, I tell ye! (*pulls Mrs. Alden's nose*) D'ye intend to mind or not?. (*Mrs: Alden pushes her off*) Not much ye don't do that, if I'm myself. (*about to seize her by the hair*) I'll make ye———

Harold. Hold on, Biddy———

Bid. That's jest what I'm about to do, sir.

Harold. But wait before you proceed, and I will find out whether she has changed her mind about marrying me. (*to Mrs. Alden*) How is it, my lady; have you decided to join yourself to me, and become happy?

Mrs A. (*firmly*) No, never!

Harold. Very well, Biddy will change your mind.

Bid. All right, sir, that'll please me. (*puts her face close to Mrs. Alden's*) Ye're a ragged, contemptible lookin' owld baste. Don't ye wish ye could afford to wear as good clothes as I ken?

Harold. Tell her about things that happened when you worked for her; how she used to boss you, and make you do all manner of drudgery.

Bid. Ah, yes! D'ye recollect when ye left some dirty work for me to do one day, und how I slyed yer childers away from ye? Yer family is all dead; I have been the cause of it. Ain't ye sorry ye trated me so cruelly, now? Spake out! (*waits a moment, then about to strike her.*

Harold. Wait, Biddy, I'll go and bring in the rope, and we will bind and gag her, and leave her here to starve unless she consents to marry me. She seems to have changed since I was here before. I don't know what has come across her. Perhaps a few days of starvation will induce her to act in accordance with my wishes. I'll find out what is the matter with her.

(*exit* c., *to soon return with a rope.*

Mrs A. (*aside*) I think he will.

Bid. I promised myself once that I'd have my vengeance onto ye sometime, and now I've the chance. Trate me like a dog, will ye! (*shakes her fist*) Ah-h-h-h, I ain't forgot it. If I'd know'd ye'd been here I should hev been here, and given ye hail columby, more'n once. It's rather fortunate that Harold come and got me.

Mrs A. Yes, Biddy, it is very fortunate you are here at this time.

Bid. Hoo-o-o! ye can spake, can't ye? It's fortunate for me, as ye'll soon find out, but it's rather unfortunate for ye. (*grasps Mrs. Alden by the hair with one hand, and puts her fist in her face*) Shall I punch ye right in yer nose? Hey? Ye owld baste! (*places her face close to Mrs. Alden's*) Don't ye wish ye had the grand things ye once possessed?

Enter Harold, c., *with a rope.*

Harold. That is right, Biddy, torment her all you can. She don't appear to be affected by our presence here; but she knows she might as well take it one way as another, and so tries to conceal her feelings, although in exquisite misery all the time. We will tie her hands first.

(*about to tie her, but is interrupted by*

Mr. Alden, Harry and Nellie, who enter L.

Mr A. My friend, I guess you have proceeded far enough with that! Stop just where you are! Don't you move out of your tracks!

Harold. Who are you? What right have you to interfere with my business?

Mr A. You will very soon find out who I am, and what my rights are. Edward Harold, my wife has born your abuse long enough. The time is at hand when it must cease. You have had your time, now I shall have mine.

Harold. (*placing hand over his eyes*) Can it be that James Alden lives, and appears here to overturn my plans! (*to Mr. Alden*) Who are they? From what place did they come?

Har. We did not come from the South Pacific, sir, where you intended we should perish. We have been more fortunate than that, and stand here now, to show you that your plans are all broken, and to defend her, whom you have so cruelly persecuted, during our absence. Nellie, there is Biddy now.

Harold. (*aside, and confused*) Have those children risen from the dead too? I cannot understand this. What course shall I pursue? (*to Biddy*) I guess it is time we were going, Biddy, it is getting rather late.

Harold and Biddy about to exit c. Mr. Alden seizes him by the coat collar and throws him to the floor. Harry prevents Biddy from escaping, she resists.

Mr A. No my good fellow, you must stay here for the present.

Har. I don't believe I'd leave on so short notice as that. We are going to settle this matter soon.

Harold. (*rising to his feet and clenching his fist*) There is one alternative, at least. Although you live, and have accidently found your wife, and you are now in her presence, that circumstance will afford you little pleasure; for her life is still in my hands; she must die by my hand before your very eyes. (*draws revolver on Mrs. Alden, it is wrenched from him by Mr. Alden.*

Larrie, dressed the same as in act second, appears in the door at c., lantern in hand.

Lar. (*aside*) Be gory! I wonder what the rumpus is about here,

Mr A. It does not belong to you, sir, to make me and my family twice miserable, by such a fiendish act. Even this crime, attempted by you, will be sufficient to send you to the penitentiary; time will verify this. The same rope which you intended should hold my wife in subjection, will serve a like office upon you. (*assisted by Harry, he binds Harold, who resists them.*

Bid. (*speaking very fast*) O, I never see sech heartless craitchers in all me life. Here I hev to bear my own burdens and others too, and then to be trated in this way. I've always seen trouble iver since I wuz five years old. I niver was an evil-disposed craitcher, as every one knows. Why was it my fate to be met here by these cruel, overbearin' folks? This hateful family was forever pokin' their dirty work onto me, and I thought I'd got rid on 'em, but now, they must stick their dirty noses in here now, and spile everything. I feel as if this is the death stroke to me; I know it is, I know it is. O dear, have mercy on a poor innocent out-cast. Take pity and relave her in her wretchedness. Boohoo-o-o!

Lar. (*aside—who has been watching operations*) Sure and that sounds as Biddy used to! Perhaps 'tis her, and them two youngsters are the children I'm in search of, who knows?—Hoo-oo-o-o! What a purty fule ye are, Larrie! How can it be them, since they're only eight years old. Ye're not so aisily fuled as that, are ye? I don'no whether it's best for me to go in there, or not, may be they'd sarve me as they did that chap.

Mr. A. (*having finished binding Harold*) There, sir, we will not be troubled by your operations any more. (*to Harry*) Who is this woman he has brought with him?

Harry. Why, your old housekeeper. Don't you remember her?

Mr. A. Housekeeper! Ah, yes; she is a prominent one in this affair, too, is she?

Harry. Well, I should think she was. She is Harold's co-partner.

Mr. A. She, too, deserves punishment, does she? Keep a sharp look-out and prevent her escape.

Lar. (*aside*) What did he say? Harold's co-partner! Harold! I knew a Harold once—he took those youngsters off, I'm lookin' arter. But that aint him, I guess. Don't be fuled by appearances, Larry—let's take a look at that woman, (*puts head cautiously in, and looks at her*) Be me sowl! she surely resembles Biddy! She does look desperately like herself. This is a mighty queer cohappenstance, I'll venture in, at least, and try me luck (*enters*) Gude evening to ye all, me friends!

Mr A. Who's that?

Mrs A. What?

Nel. Some one shipwrecked!

Har. What now!

Bid. (*screams*)

Lar. Don't be scared, I jist called to see if ye'd seen anything of a lad or a lassie nine years old—I've been lookin' arter 'em this twenty years: thus far, my search has been grievously unsuccessful. Can ye give me any information concerning them?

Together. (*aside*)
Mrs A. Larry!
Mr A. Larry!
Har. Larry!
Nel. Larry!

Mr A. (*advancing towards him*) Why sir, you are——

Lar. (*setting down lantern, and doubling up his fist*) Howld on, sir, hands off! I'm a most desperate man, sir! I niver got caught in a box yet, and I'm not goin' to be trapped here.

Mr A. Whose children are you searching for?

Lar. Indade sir, the Cap'n's—Cap'n Alden's! I promised him once I'd be faithful, and I'm a goin' to be, too.

Mr A. Those for whom you are searching, are before your eyes.

Lar. Before me eyes! I fail to see 'em, sir. (*tapping Mr A. on the shoulder*) Ah-h-h-h--h ye're not sharp enough to catch me there, sir. The youngsters I'm lookin' for, are only nine years old. I guess ye'll not get any ropes round my legs to-night.

Mr A. No, no, we don't want to do that. You are Larry Linegan, are you not?

Lar. That's what they call me, sir.

Mr A. You are looking for Nellie and Harry, are you not?

Lar. Yes, sir, that I am.

Mr A. Your search has not been in vain. They are here. They have been rescued by a kind providence. Nellie and Harry were nine years old twenty years ago; that would make them twenty-nine years old now.

Lar. O, sure and I hadn't thought o' that before, I know twenty and nine make twenty-nine. Let me put on me glasses and take a look at 'em. (*puts on glasses, goes close to them, gazes first at one then at the other*) I'm sure there's a sort o' family resemblance there yet, but ye see, I've been almost caught so many times that I was lookin' out for it here. I came within one of not coming in at all, after I see ye fastening that chap. (*goes up to Harold*) And this is what you call Harold, is it? (*shakes fist in Harold's face*) Ah-h-h-h-h, the villain is caught—but Biddy, where is she? O, here she is! How d'ye do, Biddy? How d'ye fale over this?

Bid. (*fiercely*) Shet yer head, ye infarnel, dirty, contimptable, smut-faced upstart!

Lar. (*laughing*) O, that sounds natural! I thought it was you, Biddy, before I come in, I'll say no more to ye. It seems mighty sthrange to me that we should meet here in this way. But ye see, the Cap'n told me to take gude care of his family, and arter the little ones were taken, I set out lookin' arter 'em. To-night I was at my search as usual, and seeing this forlorn looking place, I thought "twould be best to come here and look; and we can all see the result.

Mr A. I guess you don't me, do you?

Lar. Know ye! No I niver see ye before as I know of. How d'ye come mixed up in this fracas?

Mr A. Don't you know your best friend? I am Captain Alden.

Lar. Git out! Cap'n Alden sunk to the bottom of the sea years ago.

Mr A. I came very near it Larry, but have been preserved through these long years.

Lar. Presarved! Shure and I niver heard that water was gude to presarve folks in before. But, sir, ye must have been puffed up horribly big to whin ye come out, the coroner and his jury must have had to set on ye a long time to take the bloat out.

Mr A. No, no, Larrie I did not go to the bottom ; I floated on a piece of the wreck, and at last reached the shore.

Lar. O, be jabers, I see through it now, it's mighty sthrange ye should come here the same time I did. If the misthress were only here, the family would be complate.

Mr A. Here she is.

Lar. Here! I niver in all my life see the like o' this, I feel so happy I could jump over the moon.

Har. Many thanks to you, Larrie, for your persevering search for Nellie and me. We were taken away by that villain, Harold, and placed in the care of a miserable old man and woman—from there we were taken by the same vile man and placed on board a ship, that was going to the South Pacific : but before we reached our destination, the man in whose care we were, fell overboard and was drowned. We were then kindly cared for by a gentleman to whom we told our story, who took us to his home in Belgium ; educated us, and furnished us with money, by means of which we could return, and search for our friends. But Mr Alden can tell a still more eventful story.

Mr A. Yes, it was my fate to be shipwrecked ; and fall into the hands of savages, on an island in mid ocean, where ships seldom stop. Here I was compelled to serve as a slave ; words fail to convey an idea of my sufferings there : those only who have experienced the awful reality can have a conception of them. I had tried all manner of expedients by which I might gain my freedom. The savages had made promises which they said they would fulfil when I had performed a certain amount of work which they, on account of ignorance, were unable to do ; but the fulfilment of these never came. One evening just before sunset, I chanced to spy a sail at great distance, I set out for it in a small skiff. The desire of once more seeing my family soon began to burn more intensely ; the determination to leave the island, even if to find a watery grave, becoming stronger. A short time afterwards when all were retiring for the night, and my keeper came to confine me, I was ready for him ; with one blow of a missil lying near, I knocked him senseless, and made my escape in safety. I rowed vigorously for the ship, and at last reached it, and was taken on board That very same vessel proved to be the one on which Nellie and Harry were returning home ; and which foundered and we were cast adrift here in this lonesome region. Larrie you have been faithful to the last moment ; for this you shall have your reward. I shall soon make an effort to recover my property which that base wretch has taken away from us, of this you shall have a share.

Lar. Much obliged to ye, Cap'n but I can support myself.

Nel. O, Mother ! I have something to tell you. (*goes and whispers to her*

Mrs A. Very well, I am satisfied with that. Speak to your father.

Nellie whispers to him

Mr A. Yes, no one can be more willing than I. (*to Harry*) Harry, to you I am under obligations for so faithfully protecting my daughter, as a reward for this, she shall belong to you. Of her, you are entirely worthy, take her, she is yours.

Mrs A. I once anticipated that it would sometime be well for me that I took Harry into our family. Without his presence with Nellie, and his care of her during these long, dreary years, perhaps I would not see her now, and by receiving him as a member of our family years ago, I now have the pleasure of receiving him as a husband for Nellie, a son of whom I may justly be proud.

Lar. W-e-l-l w-e-l-l! Faith, and they didn't look hardly big enough to do that, the last time I see 'em. It's all right though, I endorse that too ; I always belaved in that myself, but I niver found anybody gude enough for me yet, or else I could niver get up pluck enough to ask 'em, I don't know which.

Har. I trust you will yet find some one to suit you, Larrie.

Mr A. It affords me the greatest pleasure to be again in the presence of my family. Torn from one another when life was sweet, placed in misery which could hardly be endured, and when almost——

Lar. (*breaking in*) Beg pardon, sir, for interrupting ye, but hould on a brafe moment, I've a word to say before ye finish.

       (*raises fist even with his head, and attempts to be poetic*
Advirsity's whirlwinds have hovered around,
With their dark colored wings, they sent forth full many a beastly
 sound;
But when their wings were broke and they, no longer could fly,
Be jabers—the sunshine broke forth, and we've met here rejoicing, and
I've a notion to be up and hit Harold right in the eye. (*bows to Mr. A.*

Mr A. Let us all be thankful that we are again together, and have the satisfaction that our persecutors will now suffer the penalty which they Just-·
 y deserve.
1

R. *Harry. Nellie, Biddy near* C. *Harold lying on floor front* C. *Mr. and Mrs
    Alden, and Larrie,* L.

CURTAIN.

———

· N. B. Companies who wish, can change the wording of the Play in the last act, so as to make Harry and Nellie about twenty years of age.

To Our Customers.

Amateur companies frequently have trouble in procuring Plays well adapted to their wants, frequently ordering perhaps five dollars worth in single copies, before anything suitable can be found. All this can be done away with. Our catalogue embraces plays suitable for any and all companies, and if our friends will write to us, stating the requirments of their companies, there need be no trouble in this line, at least. If a temperanc society wants plays, we have something for them. If a company wants something which is very funny, we can suit them, In fact we have dramas, farces, comedies and tragedies, which *will* suit you. Enclose 15 cents per copy for as many sample copies as you may need, and we guarantee to suit you, if you will state the size of your company, and whether best adapted to the serious or funny. Give us a trial, at least.
         A. D. AMES, Pub., Clyde, Ohio.·

AMES' SERIES OF
STANDARD AND MINOR DRAMA.

—o—

READ THESE INSTRUCTIONS.

No plays exchanged.
  No plays sent C. O. D.
    No orders filled without the cash.
      No discounts on a number of plays.
        No plays sent subject to return.

In remiting, send Post office order if possible, otherwise send a registered letter, or draft on New York. Small amounts may be sent in 1, 2, or 3 cent postage stamps with but little risk.

Do not waste your own, and our time by asking us if we can send you a certain play, but enclose your money, 15 cents per copy. If it is published we will send it, otherwise we will notify you, and you can instruct us to send something else, or return the money.

Please notice that we will not fill orders by telegraph, from parties unknown to us, and will not send plays to any one C. O. D.

A complete descriptive Catalogue, giving the number and description of characters, description of scenery, and a brief synopsis of the plot, will be sent free to any one.

Our books may be ordered from any respectable bookseller in the United States and Canada. However if you have trouble in getting "Ames' Edition" send directly to us.

A. D. AMES, PUBLISHE

OUR BUSINESS—WHAT WE DO.

PLAYS. We sell everything in the line of dramas and farces, and call the attention of our numerous patrons to our own list. We think it embraces play which will suit either professional or amateur companies. If however you need something, published elsewhere, do not hesitate to send us your orders—our stock is very large, and we fill promptly.—Stocks of every publisher on hand.

LETTERS OF INQUIRY answered promptly, and we solicit correspondence. If the business upon which you write concerns you alone, enclose a 3 cent stamp for reply. Amateurs who are puzzled upon any questions relative to the stage will be answered explicitly, and to the best of our ability.

MANUSCRIPT PLAYS. Parties who have Mss. to dispose of should write to us. We will publish whatever may be meritorious, on terms which will be satisfactory.

SHEET MUSIC. Orders for sheet music, or music books will be received and filled as promptly as possible.

CATALOGUES will be sent free to any address. Send a postal card, with your address, and the catalogue will be sent by the next mail.

HOW TO ORDER. It would perhaps seem to every one that any directions as to 'how to order' plays was entirely superfluous; but not so. We have many instances, and remember to have been severely censured by parties, some of whom failed to sign their name to their order, or failed to write the state, etc. In the first place, begin your order with the name of your post office, county and state. If you order from our list, it is not necessary to designate, only by giving the name of the play; but if from the lists of other publishers, state the publishers name, if you know it. Do not write your letters of inquiry on the same sheet with your orders, and make the order *always* as brief as possible. When completed *do not fail to sign your name very plainly..* Attention to these rules will insure the filling of your orders, by return mail. Postage stamps of the denomination of 1, 2 and 3 cents, will be taken in any amount less than $3.00.

PLAYS TO SUIT COMPANIES. Amateur companies frequently have trouble in procuring Plays well adapted to their wants, frequently ordering perhaps five dollar's worth in single copies, before anything suitable can be found. All this can be done away with. Our catalogue embraces plays suitable for any and all companies, and if our friends will write to us, stating the requirements of their companies, there need be no trouble, in this line at least. If a temperance society wants plays, we have something for them. If a company wants something which is very funny, we can suit them. In fact, we have dramas, farces, tragedies and comedies which *will* suit you. Enclose 15 cents per copy, for as many copies as you may need, and we guarantee to suit you, if you will state the size of your company, and wheth r best adopted to the serious or funny. Give us a trial at least.

MAGNESIUM TABLEAU LIGHTS. There is scarcely a person who has not been annoyed by the smoking of colored fires, which are so often used on tableaux, and whole scenes in dramas have been ruined by the coughing and noise always attendant on their use. We earnestly recommend the use of the Magnesium lights. They can be ignited with a common match, and burn with wonderful brilliancy. There is no danger in their use; they make no smoke and are cheap. Price, 25 cents each, by mail, post paid. Those who do not know how to burn them, will be instructed by addressing the publisher.

CPSIA information can be obtained
at www.ICGtesting.com
Printed in the USA
BVHW041323281218
536518BV00015B/74/P